HOT DOG! 4

GAME TIME!

Text copyright © 2018 by Anh Do
Illustrations by Dan McGuiness

All rights reserved. Published by Scholastic Inc., *Publishers since 1920.*
SCHOLASTIC and associated logos are trademarks and/or registered trademarks of
Scholastic Inc.

The publisher does not have any control over and does not assume any
responsibility for author or third-party websites or their content.

ISBN 978-1-338-58724-1

10 9 8 7 6 5 4 3 2 1   21 22 23 24 25

Printed in the U.S.A.   23
This edition first printing 2021

Typeset in YWFT Mullino.

1 2020

ANH DO

ILLUSTRATED BY
DAN McGUINESS

GAME TIME!

Scholastic Inc.

ONE

I'm Hotdog.

These are my friends, Kev . . .

HELLO.

and Lizzie.

HEY!

Some of our **favorite days** together are spent hanging out at the **park**.

I love playing **Frisbee**. Though I'm small, I can leap pretty high!

Lizzie's **REALLY FAST**. She's so fast that when she turns off the light at night she makes it to bed before it gets dark!

CLICK!

Kev isn't great at leaping . . .

Or racing . . .

But Kev is **SUPER STRONG**. He can even open those super tough bags of chips.

Together, we make a **great team**.

Kev's been missing his mom lately.

But the thing is, Kev's mom is a doctor who lives really, **REALLY** far away. She lives on **Rainbow Island**, where she looks after sick animals.

YOU'LL NEED A VERY, VERY, VERY BIG COUGH DROP FOR THAT SORE THROAT!

Lizzie and I have tried all sorts of things to cheer him up.

We **cooked** all his **favorite foods**.

But he barely even sniffed them!

We **dressed up** as his favorite foods to make him smile!

Still nothing!

Nothing could turn that **FROWN UPSIDE DOWN!**

"Why don't we visit your mom?" I said to Kev.

"Yeah!" said Lizzie. "I've never been to Rainbow Island. Let's go!"

"Rainbow Island is really far away," said Kev. "Really, really, **REALLY** far. It costs a lot of money to get there."

TOO MUCH MONEY. . .

"Don't worry, Kev," said Lizzie. "Hotdog will think of something. He's the smartest animal I know. He's even smarter than **Owlbert Einstein!**"

$$E = MC^2$$

Hmm. My brain started **buzzing**, trying to think of ways we could afford to fly to Rainbow Island . . .

. . . but I wasn't coming up with anything!

TWO

Lizzie and I were taking Kev to the park when suddenly he jumped up and shouted...

We **skidded** to a stop!

"You guys!" Kev shouted. "Look at that poster!"

Kev was pointing to a **poster** pinned to a tree.

GAME DAY IS COMING!

Teams of three compete for the **BIG** prize!

A TRIP TO RAINBOW ISLAND!

Show us your **SKILL**, show us your **SPEED**, show us your **STRENGTH!**

ENTER NOW!

"Win a trip to Rainbow Island!" shrieked Kev. "That's where my mom is!"

Could **WE** possibly enter **Game Day?** Did the three of us have a chance of winning that prize?

Kev looked **SO** hopeful and excited.

And Lizzie looked ready to take on the world, as usual.

Skill. Speed. Strength . . .

They were right.

We make the **best team** around!

We **raced** to the park!

We had **one week** to get ready for Game Day!

I was going to work on **SKILL**.

Lizzie was going to work on **SPEED**.

And Kev was going to work on
STRENGTH.

It looked like there were some other
teams at the park that were training too.

There was a team of **pigs** in mud.

SPLISH!

And a team of **penguins**.

SPLASH!

And a very tough-looking team of bulldogs. **Bob**, **Billy**, and **Billy-Bob**.

The bulldogs looked very **skillful**.
Very **speedy**. And very **strong**.

HMM,
THOSE GUYS
LOOK HARD
TO BEAT.

"All the more reason for **US** to train
even harder!" said Kev.

Kev was right. We had to work **SUPER
HARD** if we wanted to win the trip to
Rainbow Island!

THREE

Over the next few days, we trained harder than ever before!

Every morning, we **jogged** to the park together.

I was going to enter the **Long jump** and the **archery** contests.

So I had to practice my **Leaping** . . .

WOW, LOOK AT THAT GUY LEAP!

And my **aim**.

Lizzie was going to enter the **judo** competition and the **rowing** contest.

For judo training, Kev helped out as her partner.

Lizzie was like a **ROCKET** on the lake.
She was gaining speed every day!

Kev was going to enter the most events of all.

The **javelin, gymnastics, AND weight lifting** contests.

He was so strong, he could **throw a javelin** really far.

Sometimes a little **too far** . . .

Kev wasn't great at **gymnastics** to begin with . . .

The first time he tried a **cartwheel**, he lost control and **spun** into the lake!

And he couldn't get the hang of the
balance beam at all!

But after a few days he **surprised** us!

SCORE?

"10!" Lizzie and I shouted.

Lastly, he had to train for **weight lifting**.

He lifted **me**. He lifted **Lizzie**. He lifted **me and Lizzie**.

He'd almost run out of things to lift . . .

. . . when his **BIGGEST CHALLENGE** came along.

An elephant in the park **accidentally tripped** over a rock and landed on a poor pair of pigs!

YELP!

The final part of the **GAME DAY** competition was going to be the big **TEAM RELAY RACE**. All three of us would race together, passing a baton, one by one.

We were counting on speedy Lizzie to get us over the finish line first!

We were practicing our baton passing with a **long bread stick**.

I had to run first, then pass the **baton** to Kev.

Kev would run, then pass the baton to Lizzie.

GO, KEV!

But Kev kept **EATING** our "baton" before he reached Lizzie!

MUNCH!

KEV! STOP EATING THE BATON!

"Oops," he said. "It just smelled so good."

"Let's try again," I said. "Do we have anything else we can use as a baton?"

"What about this **salami?**" said Lizzie.

SALAMI?! YUM!

"Ahhhhh, maybe not," I said.

After one whole week of training and doing our **VERY** best . . .

WE WERE READY!

FOUR

The park was **packed** for **GAME DAY!** There were **colorful flags** flying everywhere. A huge crowd had gathered to watch us all compete!

"What's in the bag?" said Lizzie. "It's huge!"

Kev **grinned** and started pulling things out of the **huge bag**.

He pulled out bottles of water, **"TO KEEP US FROM GETTING THIRSTY."**

Towels, **"FOR SWEAT."**

Loads of snacks, **"FOR ENERGY."**

Loads **MORE** snacks . . .

"FOR MORE ENERGY."

Plus a white box with a cross on it.

FIRST AID KIT. JUST IN CASE!

Just as we were starting to warm up, a loud whistle blew.

PHWEEEEEP!

GOOD MORNING, AND WELCOME TO GAME DAY!

The crowd cheered as the Game Day captain introduced the teams. All of us would be fighting for the **prize** of a trip to **Rainbow Island!**

There were lots of teams, including some we'd already seen at the park.

Like **Team Ocean**.

And **Team Mud Pie**.

Team Bulldog looked as tough as ever.

And then, of course, there was us!

TEAM RAINBOW!

I was nervous . . . because I was up first!
For the **LONG JUMP!**

Lizzie rubbed my shoulders and Kev gave me water.

I peered over at the other jumpers.

They all looked like they could leap pretty far . . . especially **Kelly the kangaroo!** Everyone was looking at her. She took some **selfies** and then popped her phone in her pouch.

But, I reminded myself, I'd trained hard for this. I'd give it everything I could!

Robbie Rabbit was up first.
He bounced up to the jumping line . . .
and **LEAPT!**

The Game Day captain measured the distance in the sand.

It was a great jump!

Next up was Pablo Pig.

Pablo grunted a few times, then set off fast! He reached the jumping line and **SOARED!** It was an even bigger jump!

I TOLD YOU PIGS COULD FLYYYYYYYYY!

Kelly Kangaroo hopped over to begin her run-up. She looked so strong . . . and so confident.

"You think that was **BIG?**" she whispered to me. "Wait till you see **MY** jump."

And with that, she bounded up to the line and . . .

OOPS!

TRIP!

She **TRIPPED** over her own big feet . . . and landed **SPLAT** in the sand.

KANGAROO-AWESOME

#LOL
#TRIPPED

Now it was **MY** turn!

"You'll be great!" yelled Lizzie and Kev.

I hoped that was true! I ran as fast as
I could, hit the line . . . and **LEAPT**
through the sky.

WEEEEEE
EEEEEEE!

I pictured myself having **wings**, like an eagle . . .

. . . and that helped me get even farther!

"He's done it!" shouted the captain.

YEAH!

There wasn't much time for celebration.
I had to get to my next event—
ARCHERY!

Again, the competition looked really
tough!

We lined up, lifted our **bows**, and aimed our **arrows**. We each had **three shots** at the **target**. My hands were shaking.

Bob the bulldog's shot was right on target. In fact, every shot was right on target. He was **amazing!**

My first two shots were pretty good too,
but just as I was about to take my final
shot, the horse beside me let out a huge

NEEEEIGGGHHH!

YIKES!

OOPS.

My arrow flew off to the left,
just missing the captain!

I **raced** over to the horse to see if he was okay.

"I accidentally flicked myself in the nose with my bow," he cried.

At that moment, Kev appeared with his **first aid kit**.

"Here," said Kev, "let me take a look at that."

After some fussing and rummaging through his kit . . . Kev had **taken care** of Harry's sore nose.

"Thanks, Kev," said Harry, "and thanks, Hotdog—sorry about ruining your last shot . . ."

"Don't worry about it," I said. "Bob the bulldog was too good anyway."

The bulldog had landed **ALL THREE** of his arrows right in the middle!

Now it was time for us to cheer on Lizzie in **her** events! First up, **JUDO!**

Lizzie wasn't scared of anyone. Not even her first competitor—a **GIRAFFE** who was ten times her size!

"Go, Lizzie!" I shouted. "You've got this!"

I was right. Lizzie **did** have it.

In the blink of an eye, she'd turned that **ENORMOUS** giraffe . . .

. . . into a **PRETZEL!**

Her next guy didn't look too worried, though.

COME AT ME!

But he **should have** been!

Lizzie had him sprawling in seconds!

Her last rival was . . .

a **teeny-tiny crab**.

But boy, did he look **cranky!**

Lizzie was in for a shock! The crab lifted her with a claw and began **swinging** her around the ring.

I DID **NOT** SEE THAT COMING!

Kev squirmed beside me. "Come on, Lizzie, **FOCUS!**" he called out.

I could see Lizzie stop and take a big breath. She must have been thinking back on all her training.

It was a tough fight . . . there was a lot
of biting and yelping and thudding . . .

YEEEE-
OOOUCCCCHH

But Lizzie came out on top!

Now we had to bolt over to the lake for Lizzie's second event—**ROWING!**

Kev and I **cheered** as loudly as we could.

The captain fired the starting gun, and the rowers were off!

Billy the bulldog shot ahead of the pack, but Lizzie wasn't too far behind . . .

But suddenly there was this huge

WHACK!

Followed by a **SPLASH!**

The big elephant who had been struggling in the tiny rowboat ... lost her balance, accidentally whipped her trunk around, and **KNOCKED** the poor penguin into the lake!

Kev jumped up with his **first aid kit**.

Lizzie, who'd almost caught up to Billy, looked back. When she saw the penguin in the water, she turned around and rowed back to help!

Lizzie rowed **faster than ever!** She **FLEW** over the water to get to the penguin, then pulled her out of the water and into her rowboat.

Then she quickly rowed to shore, where Kev and I were **ready to help**.

Kev was **amazing**. He kept Pip the penguin warm, then tended to the bump on her head.

"See?" said Kev. "All better."

THANKS, KEV.

Pip turned to Lizzie. "You could have **won** the race if you kept going . . . But instead you stopped to help me . . . and now the bulldog's the winner."

"Ah, no sweat," said Lizzie.

Lizzie **LOVED** winning, but she always knew when it was time to stop and help someone out.

"Okay, guys," said Kev, swinging his bag onto his back. "Now I have to get ready for **MY** events!"

LET'S GO!

FIVE

Kev was **SWEATING**, waiting for his javelin event to begin.

"Take it easy, big guy," said Lizzie. "You'll be fine."

Kangaroo was going first. She looked very **strong** and very **powerful** . . .

But her little arms didn't send the javelin very far!

PUTT.

The javelin looked way too heavy for Robbie Rabbit, but he gave it a good go!

Now it was Kev's turn. He took a deep breath, did a **funny little jig** on the spot . . .

. . . and threw the javelin as hard as he could!

SOAAAAAAAR!!!

GO, KEV!

I'M GOING TO NEED A LONGER SNAKE!

It was **amazing!** The javelin flew so far, I couldn't even see where it landed!

The captain ran off with his measuring snake . . . and about **HALF AN HOUR** later he returned.

Lizzie and I jumped for **JOY!** We were so proud of Kev!

Now we just had Billy-Bob, the third bulldog, to go. Kev's result was going to be nearly impossible to beat.

Even so, Billy–Bob ran up to the line and threw the javelin hard into the air.

WHOOOOOSH!

It sailed through the sky . . . but didn't go anywhere **near** as far as Kev's throw!

"Kev, you're the winner!" the captain announced. **YAY!**

Would you believe it, Kev was just as amazing in **gymnastics!**

"My secret is to imagine all my **favorite** types of food when I'm competing," said Kev. "When I'm on the bars I imagine I'm a **kebab getting roasted** on the grill."

"And when I **twirl** the **ribbons** I imagine I'm decorating **cupcakes** with icing!"

The others were pretty good too.

But no one could top Kev's performance.

Now all Kev had left to compete in was **Weight Lifting!** His strongest event of all! We couldn't **wait** to see him blow everyone away.

BUT!

Just as Kev was about to lift his weights, there was a **HUGE THUD** behind him, followed by **MOANING** ...

While warming up, poor Humpty the camel had **slipped** and **dropped** his barbell between his humps!

He was **STUCK!**

Kev, mid-lift, put down his weights and **RAN** to help.

With a **MIGHTY** effort, Kev lifted the weights right up and off the camel.

"Thank you," whimpered Humpty. "That was **way too heavy** for me, and I lost my grip. You saved me, Kev."

"Ah, it was nothing," said Kev as he helped the camel up and gave him some water.

YOU'RE THE STRONGEST ONE HERE, KEV!

Humpty was right. Kev was the **strongest** by far. But he'd put down his weights mid-lift, so he was out of the running . . .

The win went to Billy-Bob instead.

"Don't worry, Kev," I said. "You did the right thing, **AND** you saved your strength for our last chance to win some points . . . the **GAME DAY TEAM RELAY RACE!**"

Everyone lined up, hoping this was the race that was going to get them enough points for the **OVERALL WIN!**

"We're here because we're an awesome team," I said to my friends, "and we want to **WIN** for **KEV** and his mom. Let's give it everything we've got . . . and hopefully we'll make it across the finish line as the **GAME DAY WINNERS!**"

"And don't eat the baton!" Lizzie said to Kev.

We walked to our starting positions.

I was running **first**.

The Game Day captain lifted his starting gun. "On your marks . . . get set . . . **GO!**"

I **bolted** away—my feet moving as fast as they could!

Everything was a **blur**, but when I reached Kev I could see that there were some people ahead of us, and some people behind.

GO, KEV!
RUN LIKE
THE WIND!

Kev took the baton and **sprinted** toward Lizzie. Kev's strong and determined, but not super fast ... A pair overtook him, even though he was trying his hardest.

SEE? I DIDN'T EAT IT! GO, LIZZIE!

Now it was up to Lizzie to bring it home for us ... and boy did she do just that!

She darted like an arrow to the finish line. She passed **one**, **two** other runners.

She passed
three,
four,
FIVE
runners!

It was **incredible!** And she won! By a nose!

"YOU DID IT!" Kev cried.

LIZZIE! LIZZIE! LIZZIE!

Now we just had to hope we'd done enough to win the **ultimate prize!**

SIX

It was time to find out the overall winner of **GAME DAY** and the awesome trip to Rainbow Island!

The crowd fell silent. The cameras turned to the Game Day captain for the **big announcement**.

AND THE WINNER IS . . .

The three of us put our arms around
one another, waiting for the news . . .

*PLEASE,
PLEASE,
PLEASE,
PLEASE,
PLEASE.*

But we weren't called . . .

"The winner is . . ." said the Game Day captain . . .

At first, Team Bulldog looked shocked.

When it finally hit them, the bulldogs **squealed** and began **jumping** around, **hugging** everyone in sight.

I was happy for them—they deserved to win . . . but I felt **really sad** for my friend Kev.

"Sorry, Kev," said Lizzie. "Maybe next time."

"Yeah," I added. "We did our best. You were **amazing**."

Suddenly the Game Day captain turned to Kev. The cameras followed.

"How do you feel?" he asked. "Your team was a **very close second**."

Kev blew his nose. "The Bulldogs deserve it," he said. "But I'm just so sad ... *sniff!*"

"I wanted to win **Game Day** so that I could visit my mom . . . *sniff*! She lives on **Rainbow Island**, looking after sick animals . . . My friends did everything they could to help me win . . . I just miss my mom so much!"

Silence fell across the park. And then a lot of **whispering** began.

Suddenly the **horses galloped** over.

WE'D LIKE
TO HELP.

The horses were so **thankful** for us looking after Harry when he hurt himself that they offered to give us a **ride** north toward Rainbow Island.

"We won't be able to take you all the way," they said, "but we can get you over the **mountains**."

We were **interrupted** by another group pushing through the crowd.

It was the **camels!**

WE'D LIKE TO HELP TOO.

"Kev," said Humpty, "you were so kind to me when I dropped my weights . . . we'd love to help. We can carry you and your friends through the **desert**."

And then another group **charged** toward us.

The **penguins!**

WE'D ALSO LIKE TO HELP!

"It's only fair that we return your kindness," said Pip. "We have a **boat**. We can get you across the **ocean** and all the way to **Rainbow Island**."

I couldn't believe it! Everyone was coming together to help Kev make it to his mom!

"This is the **best** day of my life," said Kev.

The crowd **cheered louder** than they had all day.

SEVEN

As promised, Harry and the horses carried us over the mountains . . .

Humpty and the camels carried us
through the desert . . .

And Pip and the penguins carried us
over the ocean . . .

... all the way to beautiful **Rainbow Island**.

It was **SO** good to see Kev and his mom together. They were so **happy** to see each other, after so long.

Kev turned to us with a **BIG SMILE**. The biggest we'd seen in a really long time.

"So many people helped me make it here today," he said.

AND I COULDN'T HAVE DONE ANY OF IT WITHOUT MY TWO BEST FRIENDS.

The three of us smiled in the sunshine.
We felt like **REAL WINNERS!**